Once there was a pencil, a lonely little pencil, and nothing else.
It lay there, which was nowhere in particular, for a long long time.
Then one day that little pencil made a move, shivered slightly,
quivered somewhat ... and began to draw.

Walker Books

PRESENTS

The

For Alvie, Ted and Ramona

MANY THANKS TO DAVID AND DANIEL.

First published 2008 by Walker Books Ltd,
87 Vauxhall Walk, London SE11 5HJ

This edition published 2018

10 9 8 7 6 5 4 3 2 1

Text © 2008 Allan Ahlberg
Illustrations © 2008 Bruce Ingman

The right of Allan Ahlberg and Bruce Ingman to be
identified as author and illustrator respectively of this
work has been asserted by them in accordance with the
Copyright, Designs and Patents Act 1988

This book has been typeset in Gill Sans MT SchoolBook

Printed in China

British Library Cataloguing in Publication Data: a
catalogue record for this book is available from the
British Library

ISBN 978-1-4063-8082-8

www.walker.co.uk

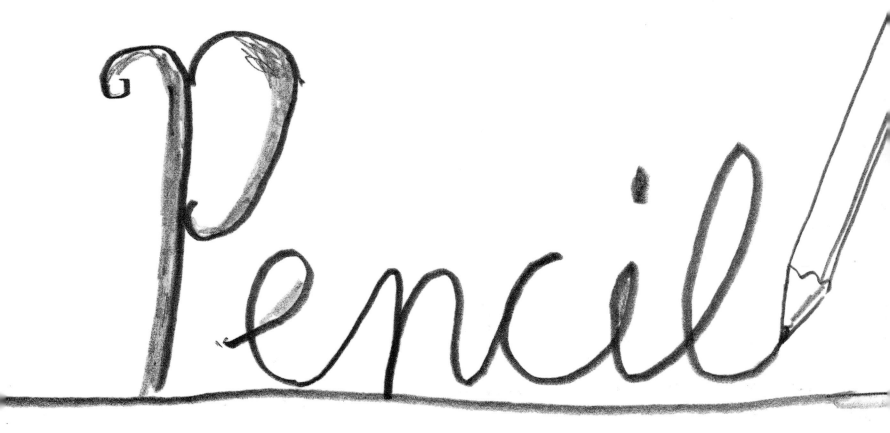

Pencil

WALKER BOOKS
AND SUBSIDIARIES
LONDON • BOSTON • SYDNEY • AUCKLAND

Allan Ahlberg • Bruce Ingman

The pencil drew a boy.

"What's my name?" said the boy.

"Er ... Banjo," said the pencil.

"Good," said Banjo. "Draw me a dog."

The pencil drew a dog.

"What's my name?" barked the dog.

"Er ... Bruce," said the pencil.

"Excellent," said Bruce. "Draw me a cat."

The pencil hesitated.

"Please!" said Bruce.

So then the pencil drew a cat (named Mildred),
and Bruce, of course, chased Mildred,

and Banjo chased Bruce,

round and round the house, which the pencil drew,
up and down the road, which the pencil drew,
and in and out of the park, which the pencil drew.

They ran around for a long long time
getting hot and bothered, tired and grumpy ...
and hungry.

"Draw me an apple," said Banjo.

"Draw me a bone," barked Bruce.

"Draw me a ... mouse?" miaowed Mildred.

"No," said the pencil. "No mouse."

"All right, cat food then," miaowed Mildred.

Only then...
"We can't eat this!"
"Apple!" yelled Banjo.
"Bone!" barked Bruce.
"Cat food!" miaowed Mildred.

"IT'S BLACK AND WHITE!"

The pencil hesitated, frowned,
looked thoughtful for a while, and drew ...

A PAINTBRUSH.

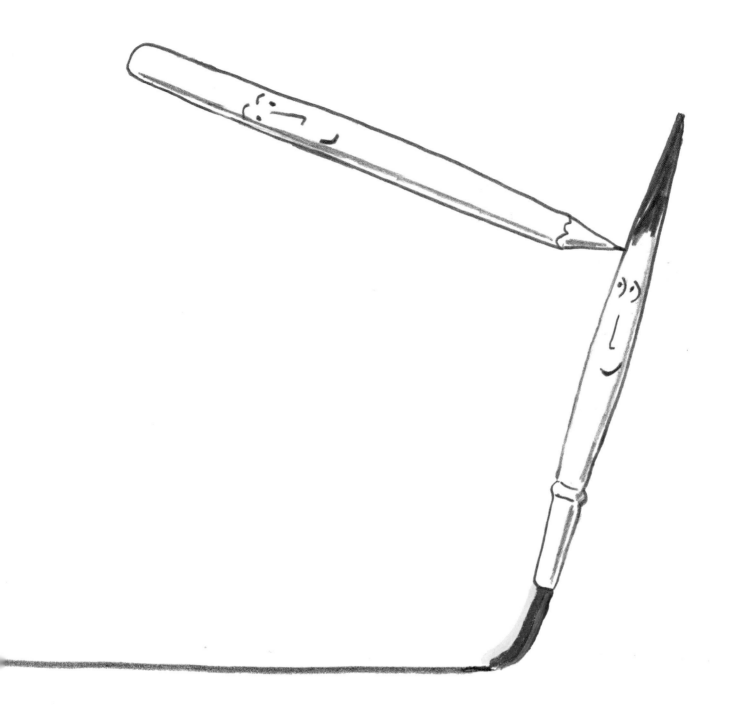

"What's my name?" said the paintbrush.
"Er … Kitty," said the pencil.
"Splendid," said Kitty. "How can I help?"

After that Kitty painted the apple and the bone and the cat food.
She painted Banjo and Bruce, but not Mildred.
Mildred was a black-and-white cat anyway.
She painted the house and the road and the park.

"What next?" cried the now cheerful and excited pencil.
"Anything!" yelled Kitty. She was excited too.
"You draw and I'll colour it!"

So they did.

Banjo got a little sister, named Elsie,
and a mum and dad, named Mr and Mrs,
some grandmas and grandpas,
three or four cousins and an Uncle Charlie.
Bruce got a friend – an Airedale named Polly –
and a ball.

"What's my name?" said the ball.

"Don't be silly," said the pencil.

 The ball made a sad face.

"All right then ... 'Sebastian'," said the pencil.

Then, all of a sudden – TROUBLE.
Banjo kicked Sebastian – "Oh!" –
into the air and broke a window.
Polly ran off with Bruce's bone.
"What's my name?" said the bone.
One of Mildred's kittens –
which she had just asked for –
got stuck up a tree.
And EVERYBODY was grumpy
and starting to complain.

"This hat looks silly," said Mrs.
"My ears are too big," said Mr.
"I shouldn't be *smoking a pipe*," said a grandpa.
"Get rid of these ridiculous trainers!" yelled Elsie.

The pencil hesitated, frowned,
looked worried for a while, quivered somewhat,
and drew ...

A RUBBER.

After that the rubber,
as you might expect,
rubbed things out —
hats and ears and such.
The pencil and the paintbrush
drew and painted them again.
Everybody was HAPPY.

Only then – MORE TROUBLE.
The rubber rubbed other things out.
(He was excited too.)

He rubbed the table out
and the chair out
and the rug out,

and the front door out,   and the house out.

He rubbed the tree out
and the kitten (who was still up it) out
and the other kittens out.
And the cousins
and the grandmas
and Uncle Charlie –

OUT! OUT! OUT!

He rubbed the road out
and the park out
and the sky out.
He rubbed everything –
even Kitty the paintbrush –
OUT!

Now once more there was only the pencil,
that lonely little pencil, and nothing else.

The rubber kept on coming.
The pencil drew a wall to stop him.
The rubber rubbed it out.

He drew a cage to keep him in.
The rubber rubbed it out.

He drew a river and some mountains,
lions and tigers and bears – "Oh, my!"
The rubber rubbed them out.

Then, when all seemed lost and there was absolutely no escape,
that brave and clever little pencil quivered somewhat,
shivered slightly, and drew ...

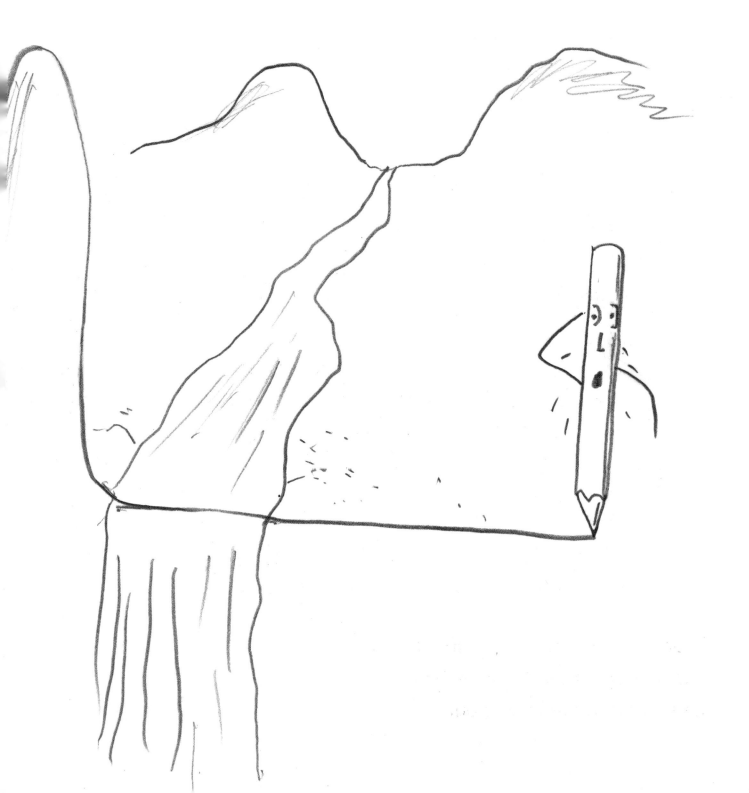

ANOTHER RUBBER.

And what did these TWO RUBBERS do?
Their names were Ronald and Rodney, by the way.
Yes, of course, as you will surely guess,
they rubbed each other ...

OUT!

After that – of course, of course! – the pencil drew
Banjo and Bruce, Mildred and the others all over again,
and Kitty – he drew her as well – coloured them in.

He put the sun back in the sky,
the house back on the road,
the kitten back up the tree,
the grass back in the park,
and a *picnic* – a lovely brand-new picnic – out on the grass.

The picnic lasted for a long long time.
Banjo played football with Sebastian – "Oh!" – and his little cousins.
Banjo's dad tried eating a boiled egg, named Billy, but it ran off.
A whole column of ants ("What're our names?" said the ants*)
came marching across the tablecloth.

*Alice,   Alvie,   Abraham,   Amy,   Araminta,   Alberic,   Algernon,   Anastasia,   Ada,   Allan...

Finally the sun went down,
the eating and the games and the adventures
came to a stop, and everybody – and everything –
went home to bed.

The pencil drew a moon in the sky
and some darkening hills.
And Kitty, the paintbrush, painted them.
He drew a snug little box with a cosy lining.
And Kitty painted that.

She painted him too.